COLD STONES
AND
OLD BONES

DAVID BRETT SAUNDERS

Books by David Brett Saunders

ROMANS & BRITONS
For Honour And Not For Glory

VIKINGS & SAXONS
All Sins Must Be Paid For

LATER MIDDLE AGES
Cast No Shadow

HIGH MIDDLE AGES
Awful The Many Foul Deeds

ROMANS & BRITONS
Cold Stones And Old Bones

Copyright © 2021 David Brett Saunders

Designed by Jeremy Paxton

Set in 11pt Palatino Linotype

Printed in the UK

All rights reserved

1 4 6 8 10 12 14 16 18

ISBN: 978-0-9567753-8-2

No part of this publication may be reproduced, stored in a retrieval system, or in any form or by any means, without the prior permission in writing of the author, nor be otherwise circulated in any form of binding or cover other than that in which it is published and without a similar condition including this condition being imposed on the subsequent publisher.

List of Contents

Dedications 2

A Literary Quote 3

List of Fictional Characters in Legio VI Victrix 4

List of Roman Forts on or near Hadrian's Wall 5

List of Roman Place Names 6

Prologue 7

Beginning 8

Part 1 – Chapters 1 to 7 – The Journey North 9

Part 2 – Chapters 8 to 13 – Building Hadrian's Wall 25

Part 3 – Chapters 14 to 23 – Manning The Wall 37

Part 4 – Chapters 24 to 32 – Trimontium And Memories 57

Ending 71

Epilogue 72

Once again being dedicated to my wife Bev and my daughters Emma, Claire and Amy

Also dedicated to all the people who are working to excavate and save and maintain Hadrian's Wall especially at Vindolanda and Housesteads Roman forts

And of course in continued remembrance of all the wonderful books of Rosemary Sutcliff

A Literary Quote

*"I am a leaf on the wind,
Watch how I soar"*

Quote from the fantastic Space Western sci-fi film "Serenity" (2005) which was a sequel of sorts to Joss Whedon's television series "Firefly" (2002)

List of Fictional Characters in Legio VI Victrix

The Legate of Legio VI – **Titus Curtius Laurentius**

Centurio Primus Pilus – **Aulus Macrinius Vivianus**

Greek Chief Medic – **Callicrates**

Friendly Centurion – **Hostus Opsidius Fabianus**

Another Centurion – **Mettius Lucilius Oppianus**

Senior Men of the 6th Century of the 4th Cohort of Legio VI Victrix:

Centurion = Century Commander – **Publius Volponius Corvus**

Optio = Second in command – position currently unfilled

Tesserarius = Watch Commander – **Quintus Annius Petronius**

Signifer = Standard Bearer – **Appius Pomponius Decianus**

Cornicen = Hornblower/Signaller – **Servius Rufius Floridus**

Conturbium or Tentful of 8 men led by the Decanus Vitus:

Tullus Vitruvius Gordianus – who is known as **Vitus**

Gaius Minucius Gratianus

Lucius Flaminius Gentilis

Marcus Vitellius Albanus

plus **Decimus, Manius, Proculus** and **Sextus**

also **Branwen** a local woman linked to Vitus and their son **Bran** later known as **Brannus**

List of Roman Forts on or near Hadrian's Wall from East to West

East	South Shields	=	**Arbeia**
(1)	Wallsend	=	**Segedunum**
(2)	Newcastle	=	**Pons Aelius**
(3)	Benwell	=	**Condercum**
(4)	Rudchester	=	**Vindobala**
(5)	Haltonchesters	=	**Onnum**
South	Corbridge	=	**Corstopitum**
(6)	Chesters	=	**Cilurnum**
(7)	Carrawburgh	=	**Brocolitia**
(8)	Housesteads	=	**Vercovicium**
South	Chesterholm	=	**Vindolanda**
(9)	Greatchesters	=	**Aesica**
"16"	Carvoran	=	**Magnis**
(10)	Birdoswald	=	**Banna**
(11)	Castlesteads	=	**Camboglanna**
(12)	Stanwix	=	**Uxelodunum**
(13)	Burgh-by-Sands	=	**Aballava**
(14)	Drumburgh	=	**Coggabata**
(15)	Bowness-on-Solway	=	**Maia**

List of Roman Place Names

Gesoriacum	=	Boulogne-sur-Mer, France
Oceanus Britannicus	=	English Channel
Rutupiae	=	Richborough
Durovernum	=	Canterbury
Londinium	=	London
Tamesis	=	River Thames
Isca	=	Caerleon, South Wales
Deva	=	Chester
Lindum	=	Lincoln
Eboracum	=	York
Cataractonium	=	Catterick
Corstopitum	=	Corbridge
Vercovicium	=	Housesteads
Trimontium	=	Three Hills, near Newstead, Scottish Borders

Prologue – AD 117 to AD 122

The great soldier Emperor Trajan, who presided over the second greatest military expansion of territory of the Roman Empire since the first Emperor Augustus, died in AD 117.

He was succeeded by his cousin and apparent nominated heir Hadrian, who was then aged 41.

Hadrian proceeded to upset the Roman Senate by abandoning Trajan's expansionist policies to seek to set up stable, defensible borders and attempt more unification of the Empire's many different peoples and try to keep the Empire intact.

Emperor Hadrian was a great traveller and he personally visited almost every province of the Empire.

The province of Britannia suffered some major unrest around AD 119 to 121 and order had needed to be restored.

Emperor Hadrian visited Britannia in AD 122 and ordered that a wall be built to limit the northern extent of the Empire and "to separate Romans from barbarians."

But as well as its defensive military role, it was also a frontier able to be monitored and allow the cross-border passage of people and livestock to be controlled and administered.

When built the wall was to be 80 Roman miles in length from Wallsend on the River Tyne in the East across to Bowness-on-Solway in the West (that is equivalent to 73 modern miles).

Historical Note: a Roman mile or "mille passum" was the equivalent of 1,000 paces; and a pace was 5 Roman feet, so a Roman mile was 5,000 feet in their length.

Beginning

**Let me tell you a story
About old friends and family
And a long wall that was built
From one side of the land to the other ...**

PART ONE
AD 122

THE JOURNEY NORTH

Chapter 1

The recruits assigned to Legio VI Victrix were assembled at the port of Gesoriacum for the sea journey over to Britannia.

Amongst them three young lads were looking about uncertainly, and in the seemingly disorganised mass of soldiers they were somehow thrown together and allocated to one of the Batavian transports being used for the crossing.

After a bit of an uncomfortable silence the three young men gradually started to talk to each other and shyly introduce themselves.

The first was a young man of medium height with black hair and a fine upright bearing – he was named Gaius Minucius Gratianus from an old patrician family but now of somewhat impoverished means. Beyond his initial reticence he looked quietly confident but not cocky and seemed to exude authority.

The second was a seemingly gentle giant of a man with thick unruly light brown hair – he was called Lucius Flaminius Gentilis and was a younger son from a family of farmers outside of Rome. He said he was good with all types of animals but didn't want to be a farmer and had wanted to see some adventure by enlisting in the army.

The third and final one was a slightly strange looking character – tall and thin and with some slight traits of a condition called Albinism in having a very fair complexion and wispy blond almost white hair and not the best of eyesight. He was named Marcus Vitellius Albanus and he also possessed a cheerful ready smile.

They helped to load up the boat with their weapons and armour and then boarded with all the other men. Most were directed below into the hold to find a place to sit down or rest amongst the cargo, although some remained on deck trying to stay out of the way of the exasperated sailors.

The heavily laden transport cast off from the jetty and all the boats set sail to cross the channel between Gaul and Britannia known as the Oceanus Britannicus.

The weather was not too bad and the sea was not all that rough so that there was not much seasickness amongst the soldiers. Still several had to rush over to the sides to retch and Marcus felt slightly queasy but managed to hold out and avoid puking.

Although the three lads didn't appear to have much in common from their different backgrounds, they were all quite companionable and excitedly looking forward to their posting to the legions in Britannia.

"I wonder where we'll be sent to?" pondered Marcus.

"I've heard that the Legio VI is said to be based further up North in the island" replied Gaius who seemed to know slightly more about the land of Britannia.

"I don't care where I end up as long as there are taverns, plenty of food and good company to while away the hours with" said Lucius.

They looked at each other and laughed heartily.

Chapter 2

And they were certainly going to have a lot of time together.

When the boats reached the other side and arrived at the large port of Rutupiae the couple of hundred recruits were swiftly offloaded and directed to the nearby camp next to the Roman fort there. After a much needed hot meal they were bedded down.

Early the next morning they were roused and after a hasty breakfast the soldiers were formed up. Under the orders of a young Tribune and several centurions they marched off on the Roman road called Watling Street westwards towards Durovernum.

They carried on past Durovernum as one of the centurions said they had to learn to march like proper legionaries and go long distances in a day.

Finally as the sun dipped low in the sky they stopped and camped near a stream that was close to the road.

Marcus took off his hob-nailed sandals and massaged his aching feet and said "I hope every day is not this tough!"

A passing centurion overheard this remark and guffawed "Boy, today was easy! Just you wait, we've got hundreds of miles more to journey before we reach our base at Eboracum. You will get accustomed to all this marching by the time we get there, and it will certainly toughen your feet up as you get used to the blisters!"

After another three more days of hard footslogging they could see the sight of Londinium laid out in front of them across the wide river Tamesis.

They crossed over the great bridge and proceeded to go around the city walls to encamp just outside them.

Londinium was nothing like the size of Rome but still lots of people could be seen bustling around going about their daily lives in the capital of Roman Britannia.

But there was no time to linger and take in the sights of the nascent, growing town as the next day they set off early northwards up the straight Roman road named Ermine Street.

They were heading on a long way up towards Lindum.

Chapter 3

Seven days more marching along Ermine Street took them to Lindum. It had been fairly up and down through flat stretches, hills and forests but just coming into Lindum they had to ascend a very steep hill to get to the camp ground up at the large flat hilltop.

They saw the Tribune going off to the fort to have a meal with the commanding officer there. The centurions left behind quickly organised them to erect tents and start cooking fires.

Any delay in acting on orders was swiftly punished by a blow from a centurion's thick vine staff – centurions had the power to discipline and hit soldiers and also even civilians as they saw fit!

The next day a slightly worse for wear and unsteady Tribune ordered them out of Lindum camp and back onto Ermine Street to travel further North onto Eboracum.

Four more days took them to the major town of Eboracum where the large fort was the main base for Legio VI Victrix.

As they approached the main entrance gate of the fort the three new friends noticed a small boy marching by their side waving a short wooden sword most vigorously.

Gaius and Marcus merrily called out to him for his bold actions.

Tall Lucius stepped out of line, without attracting the attention of any centurions, and comically advanced on the boy and engaged in mock fighting with him and then reeled away as if struck down.

The boy cheered his apparent victory.

Just then a young woman and an older Roman soldier appeared out of the gap between two ramshackle wooden huts.

The woman called out scoldingly "There you are Bran, you naughty boy; so this is where you got to, messing about and disturbing these young Roman soldiers!"

"Oh, he was no trouble at all" said Lucius.

"He seems like a fine young lad" chipped in Marcus.

"And so he is" said the bearded Roman soldier smilingly. "He is our young son and a mischievous tyke to handle. I see you have come in with the new recruits, how long have you been in Britannia?"

Gaius replied " We only arrived down at Rutupiae just fifteen days ago, and it seems like we have been marching all the time since then."

"Well at least your feet will have got used to all that marching by now."

"I don't think my feet will ever feel right again!" grumbled Marcus.

And all the others there cheerfully laughed out loud.

"My name is Vitus and I will walk on with you to the fort."

He turned to his woman and said "Goodbye, my sweet Branwen, look after yourself and young Bran until I see you again."

The woman smiled and promptly grabbed the young boy tightly and as they walked away she cajoled him to wave back to the soldiers as she did so to her man.

Chapter 4

Vitus turned away and clapped Lucius on the back "I hope for your sake that you can fight better than that when it comes to the real thing against a horde of barbarian tribesmen!"

"I hope so too" grinned Lucius.

"By the way what are your names?"

"Our names are Gaius, Lucius and Marcus" said Gaius as he pointed to each of them in turn.

"Come on then, we'd better catch up to the others" responded Vitus.

And when they did one of the centurions noticed their return "Ah, Vitus, I hope you are not leading these young men into trouble so soon!"

"Oh no, Hostus, I would never do such a thing! How are you keeping yourself, my old friend?"

"Not so old, thank you. But dusty and tired, and eager to slake my thirst on the finest wine at the centurions' mess tent. See you later, my old companion."

"With your leave can I take these three youngsters into my century?"

"I suppose so, Vitus, you did take many casualties in those last raids and I owe you one for all your bravery. I will get it so recorded and square it up with the Primus Pilus when I next see him up at Corstopitum."

"Thank you Hostus, I appreciate this."

"And so you should" replied Hostus as he strode off.

Vitus turned to the lads and said "Well that's settled then, you are joining me in the 6th Century of the 4th Cohort under the new centurion Tullus Trebonius Regulus and you shall be in my tent of eight where I am the Decanus."

"Now that you have been allocated your final postings let us find somewhere slightly better to sleep than with the unassigned recruits."

And they followed Vitus as he led them to a nearby barrack building where they dumped their equipment before going to find their evening meal.

Chapter 5

However they did not stay long in Eboracum as the bulk of the legion was further up North; and the recruits heard the first rumours that the Emperor Hadrian was proposing a major construction project.

Somehow Vitus had managed to secure all four of them a seat on the supplies piled up on one of the wagons being drawn by oxen.

"Better on the feet, eh?" grinned Vitus at them.

"Much better" smiled Marcus back at him.

So they now lumbered along another Roman road called Dere Street north westwards and passed through the fort of Cataractonium and its accompanying settlement and thence onwards towards their final destination at Corstopitum.

As the wagon finally rumbled into the fort at Corstopitum, a rugged older soldier detached himself from a group of men and came towards them and spoke up to Vitus.

"Sadly things have changed since you went down to Eboracum, Trebonius has up and left as our new centurion and Volponius has somehow got himself promoted to fill the post and is already throwing his weight about."

Vitus replied "Just the news I wanted to hear, I don't think! There is no love lost between us. Damn that man!"

"And he says he is going to leave the role of Optio vacant for the moment, when you know that by rights it should be filled by either me or you."

Vitus scowled and rubbed his chin "This is Quintus Annius Petronius, the Tesserarius of our century, and these are three new recruits who will be coming into my tent group.

As to Volponius' elevation I do not know what to say right enough – what exactly happened with Trebonius?"

"He just went in to see the Legate and then came back out and quickly packed his possessions and went off hurriedly without a word. Rumour has it that there were some money issues involved apparently – you know how rumours fly about, don't you?"

"Well, I am just going off to check up on matters with the centurion Hostus, and could you take these lads over to their new barrack room, Annius? And don't be telling them too many tales!"

"As if I would!"

And with that Vitus strode off towards the principia headquarters building.

Chapter 6

Annius shook his head and then gestured for the three friends to follow him "Not lucky with centurions, our century ain't! First Gnaeus died of the fever and then his replacement Trebonius left so very quickly."

"What more can you tell us about Vitus?" asked Gaius inquiringly.

"Vitus has been with the legion for many years, longer than me even; he joined up when it first went to Germania. He was an Optio once, brave and bold, but he got into big trouble when he disobeyed a real fool of a centurion and led the men bravely forward to stop an ambush attacking and capturing the then Legate and his friend Hostus."

"Oh that was good then" interrupted Marcus.

"But then he came back and argued violently with the centurion in public and called him a coward to his face out loud. The Legate moved the centurion on but had no choice but to demote Vitus to a foot-soldier in the circumstances."

"Vitus has ever been one to query bad orders – unfortunately whether they are good or bad sometimes does not seem to matter to those in command who wield the vine stick so harshly."

"Well here you are then, this is your barrack room, go in and meet the others and await the return of Vitus."

"By the way, you'd best watch out not to get on the wrong side of Volponius! And also be careful what you say and do in front of his toady the Signifer Pomponius as well."

They all thanked the Tesserarius for his assistance and good advice and walked on into the room.

There were four other men already in the barrack room, sitting or lying on their camp beds, who looked up as the three young men came in.

"New recruits, eh" said one.

Another tall man said "More like fresh meat for Volponius to hit with his trusty vine staff!"

"Oh shut up you two" interjected a third soldier "We're all in it together, ain't we? Sorry boys for their rudeness, I am Sextus."

"And I am Manius" said the first soldier.

"I am Proculus" said the tall man "and the quiet one over there in the corner is Decimus."

And Decimus looked up from cleaning his helmet and nodded in their direction.

Chapter 7

Thereupon Vitus walked in, red-faced and looking in a foul mood.

"I can't believe it! They've just gone and promoted Volponius to centurion when they should surely know he's not the right person to lead the men."

The other older men murmured in agreement.

"He's bad-tempered and shifty and never does the work himself but gets others to do the hard graft. Damn it!"

Just then a raven black-haired centurion appeared in the doorway of the barrack room – what he might have heard they could not know – along with a small, thin young man sticking close by the other's side.

The centurion swaggered in swishing his vine staff in the air "Ah Vitus, I see you have come back from your leave in Eboracum; I hope you enjoyed your little pleasures down there with the natives!"

"Yes, Volponius, I enjoyed my time away – and I hear congratulations are in order and that you are our new centurion."

"Just so, and things are going to change now I am in charge. Discipline was too lax in this century under Gnaeus and Trebonius but I shall wield the rod and instil some order into the men."

"I'm sure you will" replied Vitus.

"I will indeed! I see you have three new recruits in this room – why have I not been consulted in assigning them their places?"

"Centurion Hostus declared on the journey that they should all be put under my supervision following the losses of my former tentmates."

"Hostus your old friend, eh? I see you have worked things out nicely for your convenience."

Vitus visibly bristled but Volponius ignored him and turned towards the three young men.

"Well you are here now with Vitus but don't let his old tricks and dodges persuade you that you will have an easy ride. Everyone will have to buck up in my century and work hard to meet my requirements."

"Very well said, sir" piped up the sycophantic man behind him whose high-pitched voice squeaked across the room.

"This is Pomponius, the Signifer of the century, who is my eyes and ears in all manner of things."

"And also the administrator and banker of your legionary funds" chipped in the fawning little man.

"I suppose I had better leave you to settle in, and like Vitus here make sure you stick to following my orders precisely and without complaint."

And with that the two odious men slunk off out and Vitus raised his eyes to the heavens and whispered quietly "Oh Mithras, protect me from fools, and help me to keep my patience and refrain from wringing his scrawny neck!"

PART TWO
AD 122 – AD 129

BUILDING HADRIAN'S WALL

Chapter 8

The next day the Legate, Titus Curtius Laurentius, who was commander of Legio VI Victrix gathered the legionaries together and gave a rousing speech.

"The illustrious Emperor Hadrian has given us a great enterprise to undertake – to build a wall as a glorious frontier to mark the northern limits of the Empire."

"All three legions in Britannia will come together to erect a stone wall between the eastern shoreline and the coastline over in the West."

"And I expect this legion to be the best and hardest working group of men – don't let me down! Tomorrow we march East to commence building a camp from where to start work."

And so early next morning they left the fort of Corstopitum and set off eastwards towards what was to be the start location of the wall and the associated bridge to be built there called Pons Aelius.

The first planned fort to be built was scheduled to be at the edge of the large River Tyne at this place now called Newcastle.

The soldiers needed to build their encampment and worked through the afternoon to finish the turf walls surrounding the newly-pitched tents of the legionaries and the larger marquees of the commander's lodgings and headquarters.

Over the next few days the other two legions appeared and made their encampments: Legio II Augusta to the West and Legio XX Valeria Victrix slightly to the South.

The undertaking of constructing the great wall was going to be led by the engineer specialists and masons and carried out by the hardworking legionaries – but even with all the skills of the experienced Romans it was going to take years to complete.

The three young friends were amazed at all the hustle and bustle; they had never seen so many soldiers all brought together.

Vitus had to keep moving them along and stop them from gawping at some of the sights of all the men and materials gathered.

There was also the spectacle of all the eagles and standards on display within the centres of each of the encampments.

Volponius was full of his instructions, but like them all, was kept so busy by orders from above that he didn't have time to throw his weight about and come down hard on them!

Every day after a snatched early morning snack the men marched out of the camps and headed over to the extending line of wall that was steadily being added to.

Chapter 9

The great frontier wall besides being a defensive structure to keep out dangerous barbarians was also to act as a barrier to control who was allowed in or out of Britannia and was a clear statement of the might of the Roman Empire.

Hadrian's Wall as it later became known enabled the length of the frontier to be monitored and the cross-border passage of people and livestock to be controlled and then also taxed appropriately.

As there were no large natural physical boundaries it was designed to be built across the narrowest part of land between the eastern and western coastlines.

Many, many tons of stone blocks were being transported northwards from the nearest local quarries. Other stones and rubble were being collected and also the materials to make large quantities of lime mortar.

The initial plan had been to build a continuous wall of stone in the East and of turf in the West. But this plan was soon changed early on when it was decided to insert large forts into the wall itself and so more of the wall was to be constructed out of stone.

The two inner and outer walls were to be filled in between with rubble to make a hard compacted surface and then other cobblestones were to be laid on top to make a walkway.

In front of the outer wall there was to be a ditch and sometimes other defensible obstacles.

Running parallel to the wall, a little further to the South was an earthwork called the Vallum consisting of a central ditch between two mounded banks of earth. This Vallum was designed to be further protection facing to the rear.

And not far behind that was the old Roman military road originally laid down decades before known as Stanegate, useful for the quick movement of men and supplies across the wall line.

There were to be at least fourteen forts – later increased to fifteen or sixteen depending on how you viewed them as actually sitting on the wall – spread out along the wall with intended garrisons to be usually auxiliaries ranging from several hundred men to even sometimes over 500 or 600 soldiers.

Every Roman mile there were to be built small fortlets (or guardposts) known as milecastles housing about 20 to 30 or so men.

And between each pair of milecastles lay two small turrets acting as watchtowers manned by four to six sentries on a 24 hour watch system in rotation, manned by men from the nearby milecastles.

The early Broad Wall was to be 10 Roman feet wide with a maximum height of anywhere up to 15 feet depending on the terrain. Later on the width of the wall was reduced to 8 Roman feet and this was known as the Narrow Wall.

But most of this lay in the future as the rest of the wall had still to be built.

Chapter 10

But as work progressed Volponius started to make his mark on the men of Vitus' tent. He gave them extra duties and often got them to do cleaning of the latrines, which was dirty and smelly work.

Always, with the aid of his sidekick the Signifer Pomponius, he was trying to wind them up and catch them out over some ill-discipline.

Volponius was ever keen to use his vine stick to hit them as well; in particular picking on the gentle giant Lucius hoping to goad him into losing his temper and reacting so that then Volponius could really discipline and punish him.

But Vitus tried his best to look after his tent companions and stood up against Volponius, which only made him more determined to cause more trouble.

One day Volponius totally lost it with the young Cornicen Rufius.

The poor boy was cold and his lips dry and in trying to sound one of Volponius' orders by horn call, he had faltered and sounded out a wrong note.

Volponius turned on the unfortunate boy and shouted and screamed at him that he was a worthless little shit and that he would have him thrown out of the legion.

But Vitus stepped forward and ushered the young Cornicen out of the firing line as he shuddered with fear and barely suppressed tears.

Fortunately Volponius did not move forward with his threat; but Rufius steered clear of the centurion as much as he could over the next few days.

After several more weeks the Romans finished the fort at Newcastle where the engineers and legionaries also had to construct the massive bridge over the River Tyne called Pons Aelius in tribute to one of the names of Emperor Hadrian, and that was also the name then given to the location of the fort.

Chapter 11

Over time the different legions spread out and began working on different parts of the wall but in fairly close proximity.

The next forts to be built on top of the growing wall were Benwell and Rudchester.

But all this work took time and the seasons changed and passed as construction work continued.

Then the legionaries commenced the hard labour of the establishing of Haltonchesters, Chesters and Carrawburgh forts.

So over a year later they moved onto building the large fort of Housesteads which stands on the crest of one of the wave-like ridges of land which sloped up gently to fall steeply to the North, and guards one of the easiest passages through that ridge where the Knag Burn makes its way through a little defile.

The site of Housesteads was one of considerable importance for its strategic value as it was a meeting point of many roads and guarded one of the few easily practical lines for advance into the northern lands.

The configuration of the ground gave extra natural protection and the surrounding rock does come up close to the surface, but this did mean that most unusually for the wall forts that at Housesteads the long axis line of the fort was built East to West.

The internal layouts of all the wall forts follow the same general plan but all four gateways at Housesteads were large in scale and made of massive masonry.

Each stone gateway extended over the guardrooms and passages, with a flat roof which could serve as an elevated fighting platform and also catch such rain as fell to be channelled off and collected in a lead-lined stone water tank for their use.

The Knag Burn Gate just East of Housesteads Fort was unusual in that it is the only gateway on the wall which is neither part of a fort nor a milecastle.

This extra controlled gateway was probably set there to handle the extra flow of goods, animals and produce needed to come through this busy crossing point; and which in the future possibly allowed going to a regular market to be held near the developing vicus outside Housesteads.

And ultimately Housesteads was to play a large part in the future lives of some of the men of Legio VI Victrix.

Chapter 12

Time moved on and the soldiers of the Sixth Legion became thoroughly sick of the constant grind of moving stones, digging ditches and laying down walls and building the structures of the forts.

Tempers often frayed and sometimes after the day's work fights would break out between some of the legionaries.

The centurions mostly averted their gaze and allowed this to go on as a way of the men letting off steam.

But Volponius used any incident as an excuse to come down heavily and punish the men of his century – often unfairly so even if nothing much had really gone on.

He especially took pleasure in continuing to lash out with his vine rod at poor Lucius, who continued to bear this unfair treatment with stoic fortitude.

The Tesserarius Annius moaned to Vitus that their harsh treatment at the hands of Volponius seemed unfair and shabby in view of all the hard work they were doing.

But Vitus told him to be quiet as he could see the Signifer Pomponius skulking and trying to listen in and eavesdrop on their conversation, presumably to pass it all on to Volponius.

The lads of the 6th Century of the 4th Cohort just had to grin and bear it all and carry on working.

They baked in the dry summers, got wet in the rainy autumns and froze in the cold northern winters, but work on the building of the wall still progressed well due to the engineering expertise and tough discipline of the Roman legions.

Chapter 13

The forts of Greatchesters and Birdoswald were the next to be built.

Between them Carvoran, a fort that was already built and predated this great construction project, was refurbished and incorporated into the line of wall forts.

And now due to varying reasons, including the lack of nearby local stone quarries and the long length of time being taken, it was decided to complete the remainder of the long wall with it being made of high turf ramparts.

The turf wall was still an imposing structure and a strong defence, and the remaining forts were still going to be built of stone.

The final forts that needed to be constructed to complete the wall defences were Castlesteads, Stanwix, Burgh-by-Sands, Drumburgh and Bowness-on-Solway.

Stanwix was the largest fort erected on the wall, built to hold a garrison of one thousand auxiliary cavalry, the Ala Petriana known as the Frontier Wolves who regularly patrolled over the northern side of the wall.

All of this took such a long time and ultimately the three legions were working away for five or six years on the massive project.

Most parts of the wall and its defences were finally completed by some time around AD 128.

The forts and associated milecastles and turrets were garrisoned by auxiliaries of various units from many different countries of the Roman Empire.

The legions were thankful to finish the arduous task and finally get to leave and be redeployed throughout Britannia predominantly at the three main legionary fortresses.

Legio II Augusta went back down South West to the large legionary fortress at Caerleon in South Wales.

The Legio XX Valeria Victrix re-occupied Deva, that is now known as Chester.

And Legio VI Victrix was based back again in Eboracum.

PART THREE
AD 130 – AD 137

MANNING THE WALL

Chapter 14

Now the men of the Legio VI hoped that things would return to some sort of normality, but in fact a return to normal military life and parade ground exercises was all a bit of an anti-climax.

At least the building of the wall had kept them all occupied and relieved the boredom of routine military duties which dragged on when there was no fighting to be done.

Volponius continued to bear down hard on the men of his century and they resented him for it all the more. But their resentment only seemed to please him and make him even more of a martinet and bully.

Pomponius was always hanging around, keeping his ear to the ground and reporting any infractions of the rules that Volponius took great pleasure in punishing harshly.

Vitus was strong enough and experienced enough to be able to stand up to him, but the rest of the men were powerless in handling his invective and the constant chipping away at their spirits.

Eventually one man cracked and refused one of Volponius' direct orders – Volponius had him put under arrest and marched off to the guardhouse.

Discipline had to be seen to be maintained, and so the next day he was brought out in chains and taken to the parade ground where in front of all the men of the legion, he was tied to the spokes of a large wheel and viciously flogged with a cat-o'-nine-tails for one hundred lashes.

The other soldiers looked on sullenly as also many of the other centurions watched with distaste at Volponius' evident pleasure at the punishment.

This was barbaric treatment as the whip made up of nine lengths of knotted cord lashed the back of the offender tearing the skin and causing great pain.

When the sentence was completed and the man was untied from the wheel, he slumped down to the ground unconscious with his back all cut and bloody from the vicious strokes of the whip.

He was dragged away to be attended to by the Greek medics in the infirmary. The proficient care to be given by the chief medic Callicrates would be crucial to the recovery of his shattered body.

But Volponius' warped desire for brutal discipline worked against him as the men of his century stuck together and banded behind the unspoken leadership of Vitus.

Although they obeyed his further orders properly enough they also showed their contempt for him in their veiled looks and resentful attitudes.

And yet this only served to wind up Volponius more.

Chapter 15

As the number of buildings of the civilian settlements near the wall increased, Vitus' woman Branwen came up from Eboracum and along with her brother set up and ran a little tavern in the developing vicus outside of Housesteads.

It wasn't that large or fancy but it was a popular place with all the soldiers and local tradesmen in the area around the wall.

The Romans mainly drank wine which came transported from overseas in large storage jars; often this was slightly watered down to make the rougher wines more palatable.

Sometimes the soldiers and tradesmen drank beer like the native Britons and foreign auxiliaries usually did.

Slightly later the 6th Century of the 4th Cohort was sent up to assist at Housesteads Fort; and Volponius sometimes stopped in at the tavern to have a drink and ogle the servant girls.

Furthermore Volponius somehow arranged for Vitus and his tentful to be separated and split off from the other men of the century.

They were seconded on special duties for some customs work over at the separate Knag Burn Gateway, which was slightly isolated away from the fort.

Now all this might have seemed like good news for Vitus to be closer to his woman and son, but Vitus was worried about the safety and well-being of the other legionaries in the century.

He also found it to be infuriatingly frustrating to be doing what he deemed to be mere trivial customs checking of the people and goods flowing to and fro through the wall.

And it was often likely to be cold, wet and windy at that forsaken and forlorn gateway on the wall.

One day shortly thereafter a growing Bran, now aged fifteen, was wandering slightly away from the tavern in the muddy lanes near the shady side of Housesteads Fort, when he saw the centurion Volponius deep in hushed conversation with a tall red-haired tribesman with a large snake tattoo etched in blue on his right arm.

Bran kept out of sight in the shadows but wondered what was going on in their secret discussion and especially when he saw Volponius hand the other man a little leather bag containing what Bran guessed were coins.

Volponius left and headed off towards the fort and Bran watched the other man slink off and saw him join another tribesman with long moustaches who was holding onto two tribal ponies.

They rode off out of Housesteads on the little roadway leading to the Knag Burn where he knew his father would even now be working in what he guessed would be a bad-tempered and irritable mood.

The weather turned cold and the sky became overcast offering the chance of maybe some later heavy rain, and Bran returned to the tavern pondering over what he had seen.

He walked in and saw his uncle and mother's new serving girl, Fenella, clearing the wine cups from one of the tables.

Bran smiled shyly and when Fenella saw him and smiled back the youth turned red in embarrassment and swiftly rushed off towards his little sleeping area in the storeroom where the barrels of wine were stacked up as well.

"Stop mooning about and sweep the floor whilst you're in there" shouted out his mother.

Chapter 16

Later that afternoon as the day turned to dusk several of Vitus' men stood disconsolately on guard duty checking the people, wagons and livestock going through the Knag Burn Gateway.

"This wasn't what I signed up for when I became a legionary" grumbled Decimus.

"Building the wall was bad enough, but this is mindnumbingly boring checking all these native tribesmen and their scrawny animals" added Sextus.

"Well if Rome wants us to patrol this forsaken border of the Empire then I guess we will just have to do what we are ordered by our so-called betters" musingly said Proculus.

"Too true what you say, 'cause orders are orders I suppose – even if they are rubbish orders" replied Manius with a wry grin.

Finally all the traffic dried up and there were no more people seeking to enter or leave through the gate at this late hour not long before the closing and barring of the doors.

Just then, outside in the cold distance, a wildcat did growl; two riders were approaching and the wind began to howl.

The Roman soldiers' attention was slightly taken by the horsemen and they did not see the shadows of tribesmen materialising out of the darkness as they moved towards the wall and advanced along it on both sides outside of the gateway.

Suddenly an arrow thudded into the wood of one of the open doors and a wild shout was raised by about a score of warriors running swiftly to try and break through the opening.

Decimus shouted out an alarm "Attack! We are under attack!"

Battle was joined in the entrance as men lunged and stabbed with spears and swords in vicious hand-to-hand fighting.

Vitus and the others rushed out of the guardroom and piled into the fray.

It was desperate work and Proculus fell down dead transfixed by a native spear.

The weight of numbers was pushing the Romans back but the narrow width of the gateway was preventing the tribesmen from making more of their numerical advantage.

Vitus was boldly fighting and encouraging his men to hold on. The sharp pilums of the legionaries were keeping the assailants at bay.

Just then behind the Romans a couple of Hamian archers appeared and running up onto the ramparts over the gateway they started to rain arrows down onto the backs of the attacking warriors.

Chapter 17

This sudden attack on their rear broke the spirits of the barbarians and they just slightly backed away, allowing the Roman soldiers to quickly push the doors of the gateway closed, dragging aside dead bodies to finally shut the timber gates.

As more arrows continued to be shot at them the tribesmen ran off and retreated back towards the two horsemen waiting further away on the road heading North.

The red-haired taller of the two was looking on furiously as the other man with long moustaches seemed to be remonstrating with him.

Anyway with a last defiant look the horsemen turned their horses around and followed by their bedraggled men moved off northwards.

The Romans had beaten them off with the help of those two Hamian archers but at some cost.

As well as Proculus, Sextus was also dead killed by a sword thrust and Decimus was tying a rough bandage around a bad, bloody gash on Manius' left arm that would need some good doctoring soon or else things could go bad.

The archers came down the steps from the ramparts and Vitus thanked them warmly "Without your help we would have been done for – what are your names?"

"I am Hassan and this is Yussef, we were on our way with messages to the fort, but were nearby and heard the commotion so we came to help."

"Then our thanks are great and our debts to you are deep." Marcus gratefully said "Much appreciated indeed."
Gaius chipped in "You know I'm sure I've seen those two horsemen who were their leaders before. I think I saw them

once in conversation with Volponius over near the tavern. I wonder what connection he has with them?"

"I always wonder what he's up to" replied Vitus. "I had better get over to headquarters at the fort and tell them what has happened and get them to send over some replacement men to relieve us."

"Decimus, you get Manius over to the medics and the rest of you keep watch and await my return. And I will stop off at the tavern on my way back just to check if things are all right."

Gaius, Lucius and Marcus along with the two Hamian archers went up onto the ramparts above the gateway to keep a watch out towards the now empty, dark northern horizon.

Chapter 18

Over at the tavern Branwen was just ushering out the last of the customers and getting ready to close up for the night. Some of the regulars were deep in the drink, inebriated and swaying on their unsteady way out.

Her brother was away for the day, so Branwen was having to shut up on her own. Just as she was about to set the wooden beam across to bar the door, the door was thrust open and Volponius roughly pushed his way in knocking Branwen out of the way.

He seemed in a black and angry mood "Your man and his friends have been poking around in my affairs and causing trouble. Well he's being dealt with and now it's your turn to give me some fun and gratification!"

Volponius grabbed Branwen and dragged her into his foul embrace. Just then young Fenella came out from a room behind the curtained-off living quarters. She stopped open-mouthed in horror and let out a shrill scream.

Volponius shoved Branwen away and leapt at Fenella and violently lashed out at her, spinning her aside like a little rag doll to smash into one of the heavy wooden tables.

Hearing the commotion, Bran burst out of the storeroom and was confronted by a terrible scene – his mother lying stunned to one side and poor Fenella sprawled in a slowly spreading pool of blood over on the other side of the room.

Picking up a wooden stool Bran rushed and attacked the murdering villain, but Volponius was too quick and strong and fended him off and the stool was wrenched out of Bran's hands.

They locked together and wrestled, then Volponius broke free and drew his long dagger from its scabbard on his belt.

"I will gut you and then finish off your mother too, you little whelp" hissed the evil despicable centurion, "and then I will see who I can pin the crime on!" he taunted contemptuously.

They circled round and Bran desperately wondered what he could do.

The tavern room was small and compact and Bran crashed back into one of the tables; there were still some wine cups on the top and Bran picked up a couple and threw them at Volponius.

One of them hit Volponius right on the forehead and shattered into little pottery shards with the force.

Volponius shook his head to clear it and said with a venomous sneer "I will look forward to killing you, you little runt, and I shall see how long I can make you suffer!"

And with that he advanced with his dagger outstretched. Pushing Bran inexorably towards a corner of the room, Volponius slashed out with the dagger and caught Bran on the upper left arm drawing blood.

Bran used his right arm to grip his left, seeing and feeling the bright red blood trickling out between his fingers. He could sense that his end was near.

Chapter 19

Volponius moved in for the kill like a stalking lion, but then the door burst open and in came Vitus who quickly took in the whole scene laid out before him.

Drawing his own dagger Vitus advanced to engage Volponius, who suddenly looked afraid at being caught out and confronted by this equally strong man.

"You've gone too far and I see your evil hand in all the bad that has befallen us this and every day and now you will pay for all your foul crimes!" bellowed a grim-faced and steely-eyed Vitus.

The blades clashed but Vitus turned his daggerblade slightly and cut Volponius' wrist thus flicking the dagger out of his hand.

Volponius tried to turn and back away but there was nowhere for him to go and as he flailed around he lastly saw Vitus remorselessly thrusting a dagger into his ribs.

Volponius slumped to the floor with the light extinguished from his hateful eyes. An end had finally come to his bullying and reign of terror.

Vitus looked over at Bran and their eyes both turned towards Branwen; they ran over to her and picked her up and sat her down on a bench.

She was stunned and badly roughed up; Bran went and got a jug of water and wetting his neckerchief pressed the cool cloth to her head.

She started to come round a bit and saw Vitus and Bran there, "What has happened here?" she groggily managed to whisper through cracked dry lips, "Where is that horrible man?"

"Hush, hush, my dear" consolingly said Vitus "we have dealt with him and you are safe now."

"But what about Fenella?" she said clasping a hand to her head suddenly full of anxiety.

The two men turned and looked over at the poor girl who was lying quite dead.

"I am afraid that he has killed her" sadly replied her man.

Tears welled up in Bran's distraught eyes.

"What shall we do now, father?" said the shaken youngster.

"We had better get your mother more comfortably settled and then patch you up. If you are feeling well enough then I will send you over to the gateway to fetch Gaius, Lucius and Marcus and bring them back here to help us. We will have to come up with a plan as to what to do and also think of what to say."

They moved a groggy Branwen and put her into bed in one of the back rooms of the tavern.

Vitus roughly tied up the wound in Bran's left arm, and after giving him a drink of wine to fortify him then was able to send Bran on his way to get help from his tentmates.

Barring the door after his son had left, Vitus looked around at the devastation inside the tavern with broken stools and tables thrown everywhere. He sadly draped an old cloth over poor Fenella's dead body.

After going to check up on Branwen, Vitus tiredly dropped down onto a stool and put his head in his hands and ruefully cursed the fates.

Pulling himself straight he then noticed that his dagger had been damaged in the fight and that the end was broken – presumably the tip had broken off when he had thrust it into Volponius' ribs and killed him.

Chapter 20

Sometime later there was a knock on the tavern door; getting up wearily Vitus went over and shouted out "Who's there?"

"It's us – Gaius, Lucius and Marcus along with your son" said a disembodied voice from the other side of the threshold.

Recognising it, Vitus unbarred the door and let the three young men come in, with Lucius propping up an exhausted and pale Bran.

Looking at the awful mess in front of them, level-headed Gaius said "We'd better try and sort all this out before morning comes. Bran has told us what happened and all about Volponius."

Vitus pulled himself together and stood up straight.

"Volponius said to Branwen that he was having us dealt with, so it seems that he set up the ambush by the barbarians over at the gateway. But unfortunately we have no definite proof so we cannot go and denounce him to the Legate – and I have killed a centurion which is an offence punishable by death!"

"We will have to think of something" said Marcus "and Volponius was under investigation for financial and other irregularities so they knew he was dodgy."

"But they also knew we disliked him and that I have had run-ins with him before" interrupted Vitus.

"Yes, but if we can come up with a plausible story and we all stick to it, then I am sure we can bat away any accusations" responded Gaius.

Meanwhile Lucius sat Bran down behind the curtains of a back room and undid Vitus' rough attempt at a bandage. He cleaned up the wound with rough spirits and dressed it and bandaged it up much better.

Still Bran looked shocked and stunned and Lucius gently tried to lighten the atmosphere.

"There you go, youngster, you'll be as right as rain in a few days. If I say so myself I could have had a career with the medics with handiwork like that!" cheerfully declaimed Lucius.

"Only you'd make them all sick with your interminable going-on!" chuckled Marcus, who continued "anyway Bran you just rest up here for a while and try and feel a bit better."

Chapter 21

"Look I've thought about it and I've got a plan" exclaimed Gaius. "We must bury the bodies under the floor here in the back storeroom to conceal them. The poor girl had no family left and unfortunately we must also place her near that odious man."

"That doesn't really seem right and proper to me" chipped in an unhappy looking Vitus.

"I know it doesn't seem right but we simply have to hide the bodies quickly" replied Gaius.

"Then we have to make out that Volponius has just disappeared and gone off because of the allegations being made against him – and that his disappearance is proof of his guilt."

Gaius continued "And finally we also make some mention of his possible links with the native tribesmen, implying he may have even gone off northwards towards Caledonia."

So quickly the four men set to digging a hole and resting place under the floor of the back storeroom. When dug deep enough they moved the two bodies and put them into the hole – they just placed Volponius in roughly but more carefully laid out the fragile young girl.

Then they covered over the bodies with the removed earth and levelled it off and restacked the wine barrels over the freshly compacted clay floor.

Next they went back into the main tavern room and washed down the floor and furniture to remove any visible traces of blood.

They got rid of some broken stools and roughly repaired a couple of damaged tables.

When they had finished they looked around and re-appraised their work.

"It looks okay and certainly doesn't seem like there's been a fight in here" said Gaius.

"I suppose it'll do and pass inspection" replied Vitus. "I'll stay here overnight till Branwen's brother comes back tomorrow morning. I'll have to tell him what happened and they'll have to open up again tomorrow so things don't appear out of place."

"Hopefully Branwen will feel well enough to serve and they'll have to explain away Fenella's absence – say she's gone off to live with a recently found uncle in the West."

"We'll head off back to the barracks and wait for you to turn up later on in the morning" said Marcus.

Gaius added "It's been quite a day and we'll rest up till you return, and also keep an eye on Pomponius and how people react to the non-appearance of Volponius."

So the three legionaries left and went back to the fort, and Vitus popped his head through the doorway of the room where Bran was resting up.

"Well, we've sorted things out in the tavern and hopefully we'll be able to ride out the storm without too much trouble and difficult investigation."

"I'm sorry about the girl as I knew you liked her well. Rest easy and stay out of the way tomorrow. Hopefully your mother will feel better and able to help your uncle with the running of the tavern."

And with that Vitus extinguished the candle and went off to look in on his woman.

Chapter 22

Certain questions were raised by the higher brass about the disappearance of Volponius; but some credence was given to the rumours circulating that he had run off North of the wall to escape court martial for the allegations of financial misappropriation of the century's funds.

Pomponius was suspicious and gave withering and sceptical looks at the remaining men of Vitus' tent.

He seemed to sense something wasn't quite right with the whole situation, but he could not gather any evidence to dispute the stories going around.

Anyway his potential investigations were curtailed suddenly when he was put under arrest and charged with complicity in the missing money from the savings of the legionaries of his century.

Pomponius was tried and found guilty in the embezzling of funds of the legion and was dishonourably discharged and thrown out of the Roman army.

As he was escorted out of the fort he looked over at Vitus and the others with open hostility and malice, as if to say he hoped to get even somehow at sometime in the future.

Manius' arm wound eventually recovered and he rejoined his old friend Decimus back in the tent.

But other changes also soon occurred. A new centurion called Mettius Lucilius Oppianus was appointed to lead the 6th Century of the 4th Cohort and he was a good man and a brave soldier.

He quickly realised that all the men of the century looked up to Vitus and appointed him as Optio, to be his second in command for all his sound knowledge and long experience.

Vitus recommended that Gaius, although still quite young, be promoted to act as the new Decanus of the tent he was vacating – and all the remaining others agreed with that action.

Three new recruits were brought into the tent just like had happened all those years ago, and Gaius was to prove a good and solid leader of the men.

Chapter 23

They then left Housesteads Fort and went back to their legionary base at Eboracum and military life returned to normal.

Several years later in AD 135 Vitus retired after his full twenty-five years service in the army, and he and his woman Branwen settled down and opened up another tavern in the growing town down by the side of the river in Eboracum.

The following year, now aged eighteen, Bran as the son of a Roman citizen was able to join the esteemed ranks of Legio VI Victrix.

As a distinguished veteran Vitus was able to put in a good word with those in charge and Brannus, as he was now known, was put into Vitus' old century, the 6th Century of the 4th Cohort.

Furthermore Brannus happily ended up in the tent of his firm friends, the now veterans themselves Lucius and Marcus, and also under the watchful eyes of the newly appointed Optio Gaius.

Training and patrol work and more fighting were to be done over the next few years as Brannus continued to grow and fill out into a strong young legionary.

Vitus was mighty proud of his son; and Brannus had good comrades to look after him and good friends to drink with.

PART FOUR
AD 138 – AD 162

TRIMONTIUM AND MEMORIES

Chapter 24

In July AD 138 the Emperor Hadrian died at the age of 62 after several years of ill health.

His adopted heir Antoninus Pius became Emperor and ushered in a period of relative peace and stability throughout most of the Roman Empire.

It was however in Britannia that the new Emperor decided to follow a more aggressive path, with the appointment of a new Governor in AD 139 called Quintus Lollius Urbicus.

Under instructions from the Emperor, Lollius undertook an invasion of southern Caledonia winning some significant victories.

A decision was taken to construct a turf wall across what is now the central belt of Scotland from the Firth of Forth to the Firth of Clyde.

It was called the Antonine Wall and ran for 39 miles and the turf wall laid on stone foundations was over 10 feet high by about 16 feet wide.

Construction of this turf wall was first commenced in AD 142 and was eventually to take about twelve years to be fully completed.

The Antonine Wall was protected by up to 19 forts with several other small fortlets between these.

Security of the wall was improved by a deep ditch on the northern side, and it is thought that there was a wooden palisade on top, which was a wooden fence or stakewall for added defence.

Now as the northernmost frontier barrier of the Roman Empire it superseded Hadrian's Wall which was essentially abandoned as no longer required for defence or customs purposes.

But all of this was to occur over the next few years as more hard construction work lay ahead to be done by the Roman legions.

Chapter 25

Legio VI Victrix was again involved in this major construction work and some of its men were also tasked with the re-building and upgrading of the fort of Trimontium sixty miles North of Hadrian's Wall.

The status of Trimontium, so named as it was in the vicinity of the three peaks of the Eildon Hills, was constantly changing depending on the level of Roman presence in Caledonia leading to expansion, consolidation and retreats away from the site.

It had originally been built in the AD 80's and expanded, added to and then abandoned as the Romans retreated South to Hadrian's Wall, but now in the AD 140's the role of Trimontium subtly changed and became important once more.

Rebuilding work was done to slightly reduce the size of the fort which was the base for a considerable cavalry contingent.

Manufacturing and other craftwork were also being undertaken as Trimontium developed an important role as a supply and logistics centre between Eboracum in the South and the Antonine Wall further North.

All told at the zenith of its occupancy with soldiers, tradesmen, craftsmen and families and camp followers the population of the fort and associated annexes could have numbered between one thousand and two thousand people.

Chapter 26

The men of the 6th Century of the 4th Cohort were assigned to the work at Trimontium and the veterans Gaius, Lucius and Marcus along with the now experienced Brannus were heavily involved.

One day walking in the settlement outside the fort, Gaius and Marcus caught sight of a grey-haired man working at a merchant's stall who looked vaguely familiar.

The man stopped in laying out his goods and looked at them with a guarded expression.

Then the penny dropped and Gaius exclaimed "How now, is this Pomponius that I see before me?"

"Yes I am, and I am here as an accredited merchant out to sell my wares. I have no axe to grind with you lot – I have rebuilt my life honestly and fairly."

"Then we can appreciate and honour that" replied Marcus.

"The past is the past and we will not belabour it. You have paid for your indiscretions and we will say no more about them" stated Gaius.

"Then everything is fine between us" said Pomponius uncertainly.

"How long have you been up here?" asked Marcus.

"Just a few days. I am hoping to establish myself here in Trimontium to sell horse tack and harnesses to the cavalry."

"So we wish you well and may see more of you as we are currently stationed here" responded Gaius.

But in fact they did not see any more of Pomponius, as it seemed that sometime over the next few days he packed up his wares and they heard that apparently he headed back down South again.

Chapter 27

Time passed and the work of military life seemed never-ending. Things seemed to be going well for the Romans – minor skirmishes occurred with the local tribesmen but nothing of a serious nature.

Whilst the men of the legion were campaigning around this area in Caledonia, in AD 145 Brannus received word that his father Vitus had passed away down in Eboracum – the brave old soldier had had a sudden seizure and died.

Then in AD 147 after their 25 years of military service Gaius, Lucius and Marcus were able to retire and all three went to live at Eboracum in the colonia near to the major legionary fort there.

This left Brannus feeling slightly bereft and lonely, but he had the good fortune to be promoted to Optio in place of the retiring Gaius.

He wistfully thought that his father would have been very proud of this achievement.

Several years later Brannus' century was once more assigned to Trimontium to help in strengthening the guard defences of the fort.

However as the lengthy construction of the turf wall carried on, rumours of unrest amongst the local tribesmen grew and filtered through to the soldiers down at Trimontium.

The Brigantes tribe in the region North and South of the old Hadrian's Wall were unhappy with the way they felt they were being treated.

One tribal elder in the locality spoke harshly to Brannus when he was out on a patrol "You arrogant Romans always look down your noses at us and never treat us Britons fairly!"

Brannus tried to say that this was not truly so, but the old man would not listen to anything said in mitigation of the Romans and just walked off.

Chapter 28

Several weeks later whilst again out on patrol, Brannus saw a mounted tribesman talking to that old village elder, who was obviously treating the other man with deference due to his apparent high status.

Brannus looked at the horseman with long greying red-tinged hair and suddenly stopped – there on his right arm was a large snake tattoo just like he remembered seeing all those years ago down at Housesteads.

He knew all about the story of the attack on his father and friends at the Knag Burn Gateway all those years ago, and wondered that if it was the same man then what was he up to here?

The mounted man looked up and seeing the approaching squad of Roman soldiers quickly said his farewell to the elder and wheeled his horse around and rode off swiftly.

When he went back to Trimontium, Brannus recounted what he had seen to his centurion and they both wondered what this might mean and what was going on out there amongst the tribesmen of the Brigantes.

Chapter 29

Unfortunately they didn't have long before they found out – just then in AD 155 there was a major revolt by the Brigantes in the northern regions.

It was very serious and the tribes ran rampant in the lands between the two walls; the heather was set on fire and the Romans were hard pressed.

Reinforcements were badly needed to try and put down the insurrection; Legio VI Victrix came up from Eboracum along with a squad of old veterans drawn from retired legionaries including Gaius and Lucius.

The legion carried on North towards the Antonine Wall, but the volunteers were brought into the garrison holding Trimontium fort.

"It is good to see you again" said Brannus.

Gaius replied "We heard that things were bad up here so we decided to help out. I'm afraid Marcus is not too well with the ague in his bones and cannot walk far so he had to stay back home."

"I could not resist the old excitement you know" boomed Lucius slapping Brannus heavily on the back. "It feels like the good old days to have strapped on armour and be wearing a sword at my side again, although it all feels slightly heavier than I remember" and he laughed out loud.

"Well met old comrade" grinned Brannus.

The volunteers settled in and the walls were manned at all hours, and guard watches were set looking out in all directions for any approaching enemy.

Chapter 30

The next morning a great horde of tribesmen appeared from out of the mists and led by a group of horsemen advanced to attack Trimontium.

They were well organised and carried rough wooden scaling ladders and a large tree trunk to act as a battering ram.

Urged on by their leaders the tribesmen surged forward and attacked the fort at several points all at the same time.

Flaming arrows were shot up over the walls and several buildings inside were set on fire – the civilians and non-combatants were tasked with trying to put the fires out before they took hold and spread.

The barbarians suddenly broke through one of the gateways and poured into the fort.

Brannus and a group of men including Gaius and Lucius rushed over to stop them advancing further.

And in the melee of hand-to-hand fighting the action was brutal – swords hacked and spears were thrust and men on both sides fell down in the fierce combat.

From the corner of his eye Brannus saw the giant Lucius assailed by three warriors, he killed one of them with a huge sword blow but in doing so exposed his side which was then skewered by a spear and Lucius fell down dying.

Gaius and Brannus ran over to his aid and killed those other attacking tribesmen and pulled Lucius back out of the fray.

The blood was pouring out of his shattered side and they were just able to bid him farewell before he died, and then the two of them were pitched back into the heaving mass of fighting.

Chapter 31

Just then Brannus saw a tall tribal leader urging his men on with his arm up brandishing a sword – and Brannus recognised the long snake tattoo on that arm of the man he had seen previously.

Their eyes locked with mutual recognition and hostility and they advanced on each other to fight to the death for their causes.

Tiny sparks flew as their swords clashed and they thrust and parried as each tried to gain advantage and land a telling blow.

Then Brannus was backed slightly awkwardly up against a wall and the chieftain saw his chance and swiftly stabbed forward to kill him.

But Brannus turned slightly and the blow glanced off the side of his metal armour and he plunged his own sword into the rebel's chest who slumped down to the ground.

With the loss of their leader the Brigantes hesitated and the uncertainty spread and stopped them in their tracks.

The Romans rallied and pushed them back through the gateway; then the resistance of the tribesmen finally broke and they turned and fled.

Gaius and Brannus were reunited, both bloody and bowed with exhaustion and battle fatigue.

Many bodies lay strewn on the ground and hanging down from the walls, both Roman and Briton.

The slaughter had been immense and the Romans had only just prevailed and survived.

Smoke was rising up into the air from many small fires still burning in the burnt-out shells of barrack and storage buildings.

They walked over to Lucius' dead body and Gaius dully said "It is terrible to see my old comrade finally dead after all these years. I thought he was invincible and unstoppable but time has caught up with him after all and he is no more. Goodbye old friend."

And with that they picked him up and moved him away for preparing for the appropriate proper burial.

Eventually the Romans regained control and the revolt was put down – but they were badly shaken as it had been a close run thing.

Brannus was awarded a commendation for his bravery and killing the rebel chieftain in the battle at Trimontium.

Gaius said his farewells and with the surviving volunteers returned to Eboracum to take the sad news of Lucius' death back to Marcus.

Chapter 32

Life on the frontier returned to previously but there was still much tension in the air. The sullen Brigantes were still hard to handle and the Caledonians across the Antonine Wall were still proving difficult to subdue.

Brannus was starting to think about his upcoming retirement and wondering where to go and what to do.

Then in AD 161 old Antoninus Pius died and Marcus Aurelius and his adoptive brother Lucius Verus became co-Emperors.

Shortly thereafter Marcus Aurelius decided to abandon the Antonine Wall and the Caledonian Lowlands and re-consolidate back down at Hadrian's Wall which was to be re-occupied.

In AD 162 Brannus finally retired from the legions and headed down to Eboracum where he met up again with Gaius who informed him that poor Marcus had died the previous year.

They discussed about the proposed return to Hadrian's Wall and the re-activation of the forts including Housesteads.

Brannus was worried and expressed his concern that the buried bodies might be discovered in the old tavern when the vicus was also resettled.

Gaius thought about the matter and came up with a suggestion "Why don't we seek to take over the old tavern building, restock it and you become the tavern keeper. That way you will be there on site to keep things under wraps."

"That's a good idea; I would be back at my former home and near to some of my old friends in the army and I could keep control of the situation."

"Then that is what we shall do!" replied Gaius.

"So perhaps being a tavern keeper still runs in my family" chuckled Brannus.

And accordingly Gaius went up to Housesteads with Brannus to help him set up the tavern.

Firstly they laid an extra covering of more clay over the back storeroom floor for additional protection.

Then they stocked up with wines and beer just in time for the return of the auxiliary garrison to Housesteads Fort; and also the accompanying arrival of craftsmen and camp followers to the ramshackle huts of the vicus that would need much restoring and repairing.

Before Gaius left to go back to Eboracum, he and Brannus put up some carved stone memorial plaques to their old friends and family – for the former Roman soldiers and comrades Vitus, Lucius and Marcus – just as a way to honour and remember their presence at that great frontier wall in the far northern land of Britannia.

Ending

Nostalgia fills me with longing,
Yet in recalling memories
Of ones I have known and loved,
Once again happiness is reborn in my heart.

And I am resolved to make the best
Of the rest of my life,
Even if ghosts of the past still haunt me
Despite all the many years that have passed.

Epilogue

And soldiers of the Roman Empire continued to man Hadrian's Wall for nearly the next two hundred and fifty years ...

In the 1930's Professor Eric Birley and a team of archaeologists made a gruesome discovery during their excavations at Housesteads Roman Fort.

Below the floor of a building in the civilian settlement or vicus, just outside the fort, they found two skeletons.

One skeleton was of a man with the tip of a dagger in his ribs and the other, more fragmentary, was probably of a woman.

They had been buried in the clay floor underneath the rear room of what was probably a tavern, and then further concealed under another clean layer of clay.

And no one knows what might have happened back then ...

ALSO BY THIS AUTHOR...

FOR HONOUR AND NOT FOR GLORY

A young Briton, Drustan gets caught up in conflict in Britain including the AD43 Roman Invasion and ultimately the savage AD60/61 Revolt of Queen Boudica.

He encounters challenges to his honour but will not be defeated and throughout adversity he will continue to fight "For Honour And Not For Glory".

This short novelette offers up an exciting story linked to the legend of the Hallaton Helmet and hoard discovered in Leicestershire in 2000, now on display at the Market Harborough Museum.

£5.99   ISBN: 978-0-9567753-4-4

ALSO BY THIS AUTHOR...

ALL SINS MUST BE PAID FOR

Archaeologists working on the route of the Weymouth Relief Road in Dorset in 2008/2009 discovered a burial pit on Ridgeway Hill containing what turned out to be 54 dismembered skeletons and 51 skulls of Vikings executed by local Saxons.

This novelette seeks to offer a plausible tale of what could have happened at a time of great conflict in England between the Saxons under King Aethelred the Unready and the Danes led by Sweyn Forkbeard around the years AD 1002 to 1014.

It is told through the actions of Rolf, an innocent young boy who stows away on a longship heading across to England. But as the story unfolds, Rolf is drawn into a maelstrom of violence and death, and a burning need for revenge that is so all consuming that it changes him forever. And sometimes a man has to pay a heavy price to atone for all his misdeeds. But is there still a chance for redemption?

£5.99   ISBN: 978-0-9567753-5-1

ALSO BY THIS AUTHOR...

CAST NO SHADOW

Marguerite is a young girl who tragically loses all her family in rebellion and fighting in the Duchy of Gascony in France. Coming over to England in 1252 she becomes known as Margot and gets caught up in fractious strife between the barons and the king.

Along with the swordsman Jean de Savignac and the young pickpocket Tom Buckle, Margot is drawn into a web of intrigue as she plots to get the ultimate revenge she craves for. Whilst barely known to history as Margot the Spy, this spirited and quick-witted young woman has a crucial role to play in the unfolding of the dramatic action of the time.

This short novelette offers up an exciting historical story linked to the personality of Simon de Montfort and events leading up to the Second Barons' War with King Henry III and his son Prince Edward culminating in the decisive Battle of Evesham in 1265.

£5.99   ISBN: 978-0-9567753-6-8

ALSO BY THIS AUTHOR...

AWFUL THE MANY FOUL DEEDS

Rory and his younger sister Eva are orphaned in Ireland and are taken in by the kind Lady Affreca, the wife of the English ruler of much of Ulster, the famed and powerful knight John de Courcy.

But times are changing with the accession of King John, a cruel and vindictive despot who cares nothing for his subjects and the rule of law. His dangerous spitefulness will cause the downfall of many.

This short novelette goes back and forth between Ireland and Wales in the early 1200's as Rory is forced to go on the run to keep one step ahead of royal displeasure. Along the way there are friends and foes to deal with in a search for some peace and safety.

£5.99   ISBN: 978-0-9567753-7-5

David's 30 Favourite Rock & Pop Albums

1964	(01)	The Beatles	A Hard Day's Night
1976	(02)	Be-Bop Deluxe	Sunburst Finish
1971	(03)	Caravan	In The Land Of Grey And Pink
1979	(04)	Ry Cooder	Bop Till You Drop
1991	(05)	Crowded House	Woodface
1972	(06)	Deep Purple	Machine Head
1978	(07)	Dire Straits	Dire Straits
1975	(08)	Eagles	One Of These Nights
1977	(09)	Fleetwood Mac	Rumours
1970	(10)	Free	Fire And Water
1973	(11)	Rory Gallagher	Tattoo
1973	(12)	Genesis	Selling England By The Pound
1968	(13)	Jimi Hendrix	Electric Ladyland
1971	(14)	Led Zeppelin	IV (Four Symbols)
1974	(15)	Little Feat	Feats Don't Fail Me Now
1973	(16)	Lynyrd Skynyrd	Pronounced Leh-nerd Skin-nerd
1973	(17)	Pink Floyd	Dark Side Of The Moon
1975	(18)	Pink Floyd	Wish You Were Here
1972	(19)	Steely Dan	Can't Buy A Thrill
1976	(20)	Steely Dan	The Royal Scam
1976	(21)	Al Stewart	Year Of The Cat
1971	(22)	Rod Stewart	Every Picture Tells A Story
1975	(23)	10CC	How Dare You!
1971	(24)	James Taylor	Mud Slide Slim And The Blue Horizon
1994	(25)	Martin Taylor	Spirit Of Django
2005	(26)	Thunder	The Magnificent Seventh
2001	(27)	Peter White	Glow
1971	(28)	The Who	Who's Next
1972	(29)	Wishbone Ash	Argus
1986	(30)	XTC	Skylarking

David's 20 Favourite Guitarists from his Youth

b.1910	DJANGO REINHARDT	Gypsy Jazz Guitarist
b.1933	JULIAN BREAM	Classical Guitarist and Lutenist
b.1942	JIMI HENDRIX	of JIMI HENDRIX EXPERIENCE
b.1944	JIMMY PAGE	of LED ZEPPELIN
b.1945	RITCHIE BLACKMORE	of DEEP PURPLE and RAINBOW
b.1945	DANNY GATTON	Rockabilly and Redneck Jazz
b.1946	PETER GREEN	of original FLEETWOOD MAC
b.1948	RORY GALLAGHER	Irish Blues Rock Guitarist
b.1948	BILL NELSON	of BE-BOP DELUXE
b.1949	ANDREW LATIMER	of CAMEL
b.1950	ANDY POWELL	of WISHBONE ASH
b.1950	TED TURNER	of WISHBONE ASH
b.1950	PAUL KOSSOFF	of FREE
b.1951	PETER HAYCOCK	of CLIMAX BLUES BAND
b.1951	WALTER TROUT	Blues Rock Guitarist
b.1951	ROBBEN FORD	Blues, Jazz and Rock Guitarist
b.1952	GARY MOORE	Rock and Blues Guitarist
b.1953	LAURIE WISEFIELD	of WISHBONE ASH
b.1954	STEVIE RAY VAUGHAN	"SRV" Blues Rock Guitarist
b.1956	MARTIN TAYLOR	Jazz and Solo Guitarist